Mr. Jack -IN-THE- Box

JAN SPEAR

ILLUSTRATED BY
STEPHANIE GROENWOLD

ISBN: 149533581X

ISBN 13: 9781495335815

Library of Congress Control Number: 2014901791

CreateSpace, North Charleston, South Carolina

Once upon a time there was a Jack-in-the-Box.

Do you know what a Jack-in-the-Box is?

It is a toy that looks like a little boy pushed down in a box. And the boy's name is Jack.

The Jack-in-the-Box in this story ended up very lonely. He belonged to little Julie, who grew up and got married and now has a little boy named Shane.

One day when Shane was visiting his grandmother and she wasn't looking, he slipped out of sight and climbed the stairs. At the top was a door. He reached up and turned the knob. The door opened.

It was an attic! Wow! What a lot of things to explore. Shane climbed up on an old mattress and jumped on it. He ran over and looked out the window but he jumped back because he was so high up. Over in the corner he spotted a little square box with a handle. He knew just what to do with the handle.

He turned it and 'Pop Goes the Weasel' started playing. When the music stopped, the top popped open - and out jumped Jack-in-the-Box!

Shane jumped back and started to cry.

Jack-in-the-Box said, "Don't cry. I won't hurt you."

Shane stopped rubbing his eyes and looked up. "Who are you?"

"I'm Jack-in-the-Box."

"What are you doing here?"

"Your grandmother brought me up here and I've been here ever since. It's been a long time since anybody played with me."

"I'll play with you," said Shane.

"Push me back in the box and turn the handle, and I'll jump back out as many times as you want."

"Won't I hurt you?"

"Oh, no. I was made to do this."

Shane had disappeared. Grandmother started looking for him. Why was the door open at the top of the stairs? And was someone talking up there?

"Shane. Shane!"

"Hi, Grandmother."

"Are you all right? And who are you talking to?"

"Jack."

"Jack? Jack who?"

"Jack-in-the-Box."

Grandmother stepped into the attic and Jack-in-the Box said, "Hello, Granny. Long time no see."

A toy was talking! But that was impossible, Grandmother thought.

Jack said, "Would you please get me out of this attic? I've been in here for a long time. And I'm all dusty."

Grandmother did not know what to do. This couldn't be happening.

"No, you can't go out of the attic."

Shane said, "But I want to take Jack home with me."

"No, Shane, Jack must stay here - and this must be our little

4

secret. You understand? You may play with Jack-in-the-Box while you're here, but the toy must stay here. I promise to take good care of Jack until you come back."

"Why can't I take Jack home with me?"

Grandmother did not want anyone to know about a talking toy. She said, "Let's leave Jack here. You can play with him when you visit."

Jack had other ideas. He said, "I don't want to stay here. I've been here so long I feel old. I'm a toy. I want to have fun. I want to go with Shane."

After Shane left, Grandmother went back to the attic. She couldn't believe her eyes! Jack had sprouted arms and legs and was running around all over the place. He started toward the door.

Grandmother got there first. "What are you trying to do?"

"I'm trying to get out of here."

5

"Where would you go if you did get out?"

"Just around the house. I've been cooped up too long."

Grandmother tried to catch him and he dodged her. Finally she cornered him and pushed him back in the box.

"I hate to do this to you, but it's for your own good," she said.

Grandmother thought, Aha! So Jack can run around only when he's out of the box. He sure is a stubborn little toy!

She wondered if Shane would tell his mother about Jack. Oh dear! What a mess that would stir up!

The next day Julie called. "What is the matter with Shane? Ever since we got home yesterday he's been crying. He wants to go back to your house and live with you! He says he wants to play with Jack. Who is Jack?"

Grandmother sighed. "Bring Shane over and you can see for yourself."

The moment Shane got to Grandmother's house he ran up the stairs and banged on the attic door.

Julie said, "Mother, why is he trying to get into the attic?"

"You'll see."

Shane pulled Jack out of the corner, turned the handle - and out popped Jack!

"Hi, Shane. I didn't think you were ever coming back. Your mean old granny put me in the corner." Jack sprouted arms and legs and started running around the room.

Shane giggled so hard he nearly lost his breath.

Jack yelled, "I'm free again!"

Shane ran after him, caught him, pushed him in the box, turned the handle - and out popped Jack!

Grandmother said to Julie, "I couldn't tell you. You wouldn't have believed me."

Jack said, "Hi, Julie. Long time no see. You're all grown up."

Julie didn't know what to say.

"What's the matter? Cat got your tongue?"

Julie sat down on the floor. Shane sat on her lap. Jack sat on her lap, too. Julie pushed Jack in the box, turned the handle - and out popped Jack.

Julie said, "We can take you home with us, Jack."

Grandmother said, "He's got a little stubborn streak in him, and he wants to get outside."

"Oh, Mother," Julie said. "It will be okay."

8

When they got home, Shane let Jack out of the box and Jack sprouted his arms and legs. He glanced around and said, "I like it here. This is much more fun than that old attic."

At that moment, Shane's dad walked in. "Do we have company? I thought I heard a strange voice."

"You did!" exclaimed Jack. "I'm Shane's new playmate and Julie's old playmate."

Jim looked around.

Jack jumped up on a chair. "It's me. I'm a talking Jack-in-the-Box."

"He's right, Jim," said Julie. "He was my Jack-in-the-Box when I was a little girl. Mother let Shane play with him the other day and he came alive. I couldn't leave him there, so I brought him home."

Shane ran over and started playing with Jack. They scampered about all over the place, laughing and giggling.

Julie said, "Jack, you and Shane have to stop playing now. It's time for dinner."

"I'm not ready to stop," said Jack. "I'll watch while you have dinner."

"No you won't, because you'll distract Shane. Now be still so I can put you away for a little while."

But Jack took off. He yelled, "I'm not ready to be put away!"

"That's too bad, because we are ready for you to be put away. Things would be a lot better for all of us if you would listen."

Jack took off down the hallway but Jim caught him. As Jim was stuffing him into his box Jack said, "You don't understand. I've been cooped up for a long time. I want to be FREE!"

"We will let you be free," Jim said, "but you need to follow our rules. We have to make sure Shane does other things besides play with you."

"But why would he want to do anything else?"

"Shane has to live in this world. He has to know how to read, write, spell, get ready for school, and learn to play with other children. We have to make sure he does these things. Now, GOOD NIGHT."

Jack went into his box kicking and screaming. "I'll be free. You'll see!"

Julie sat on the edge of Shane's bed. "Shane, Jack has to go to sleep too. Your dad has put Jack away somewhere in the house, so don't even think about getting up and letting him out. Okay?"

"Okay, Mom."

Jasper, the family dog, heard thumping. He investigated. He went down the hallway and the thumping got louder. What was under the hall table? Some kind of fancy box. He pushed the box from under the table. The box had a handle. Jasper nudged the handle - and the lid popped open!

Jack hopped out, grew his arms and legs, and started running. Jasper growled and barked. What a commotion! Jack knew he'd better get out of there before he got locked up again. He spotted the doggie door in the kitchen and ran through it, Jasper right behind him.

"I'm free!" Jack yelled as he jumped to the grass.

Julie and Jim came running down the hall just in time to see Jack and Jasper disappear through the doggie door. Dad went outside and called Jasper in, but he didn't see Jack anywhere.

"Good!" said Jim. "He's gone. Now he won't disrupt our house anymore."

"I can't believe you're not going after him," Julie said. "Imagine how upset Shane will be."

So Jim went to look. He searched all over the neighborhood but he did not find Jack. Back home, he found Julie waiting at the kitchen table.

"Did you find him?" "No. I don't know where he is. I called and he didn't answer. Anyway, I can't find him in the dark."

Jack ran as fast as he could. After a while, he stopped. It was dark, and dogs were barking. Jack felt frightened and alone.

"I think I'll go back home. I'm not so sure I want to be free now."

But where was home? What if he never found his way home?

In the distance, there were a bunch of bright lights. "O, it's the city!" Jack exclaimed. Then he said, "I know I'm being naughty, and Shane will be upset, but I'll wait until tomorrow to find my way home."

Jack started walking and the farther he walked the farther away the city seemed. He was tired. He spotted a doghouse. He sneaked up and looked. It was empty! So he climbed inside and went to sleep. He had been asleep a while when he heard a growl. He opened his eyes. There stood a huge scary dog.

The dog demanded, "What are you doing in my house?"

Jack didn't answer.

"I asked you a question. What are you doing in my doghouse?"

Jack was shaking, but he managed to tell the dog what had happened.

"Sounds like you've been a bad little toy. You probably have those nice people worried about you. Maybe I could help you find your way home."

"Yes, they may be worried about me - but I'm going to the city. I've been cooped up a long time and I want a little adventure."

"Do you know what the city is like?"

"No. Will you go with me?"

"My name is Butch. And no, I won't go with you. It would upset

12

my owners if I just ran off. You sure I can't convince you to go home?"

"No," said Jack. I want my adventure. Can I stay here tonight?"

"All right," said Butch.

The next morning Jack set out on his adventure. Butch had decided he liked Jack, and now he decided to follow him - just in case.

Jack had never seen cars. And he didn't know about crossing at crosswalks or to wait for the light to change. He almost got run over and the blare of the car horn startled him.

A driver screeched to a stop and looked out the window.

"Look at that!" the man exclaimed to his wife. "A walking Jack-in-the Box!"

His wife didn't believe him, but she looked and saw that it really was a walking Jack-in-the-Box.

"Grab him!" the man shouted.

They both jumped out of the car. While the woman ran at Jack, the man came from behind and grabbed him.

Jack cried, "Put me down! Put me down!"

"Wow! He walks - and he talks too! We can make a lot of money with this little toy."

Butch was watching from around the corner. He saw that Jack was really in trouble now.

The man and the woman put Jack in the car and drove off. Butch followed. The car soon turned onto a side street and into a driveway. Butch lay under a big bush and waited.

The man and woman took Jack into the house and popped him out of the box. His legs sprouted and he started running around and screaming for them to let him go. He was looking for a way out when the man grabbed him and pushed him back into his box.

Jack wasn't very smart sometimes. If he had been smart, he would have kept quiet when the man took him to see the owner of a children's theater. His name was Mr. Magic, and he looked like a rabbit. He had big ears and two big front teeth!

Jack came out of the box kicking and screaming. "Let me out of here. I haven't done anything wrong. I just wanted to see the big city."

Mr. Magic said, "I don't believe this! A walking talking Jack-in-the-Box. He can perform for all the children in town and we will make lots of money."

Jack did not have any idea what money was, but he realized it was very important to these people.

Mr. Magic put him up on the theater stage and started some music. "Okay, Jack," he said, "dance to the music."

"I don't know how to dance."

"Then do some tricks."

"I don't know any tricks."

Jack panicked. How was he going to get out of this mess? He sat down, crossed his arms and legs and refused to do anything.

Mr. Magic said, "If you perform for us, we will take you to the big city."

"I don't want to go - I want to go home!"

Jack knew he was in big trouble. He had been a selfish toy. He was ashamed of his behavior, but if he ever got home again he would be a good toy and obey the rules.

16

Shane woke up that morning and hurried to play with Jack. But where was Jack? When Mom and Dad told him Jack had run away he started to cry.

Mom said, "Shane, knowing Jack, he will probably pop in any moment. In the meantime, we will keep looking for him."

Butch crouched just outside the theater door. How could he help Jack escape? Mr. Magic and the man and the woman were so busy trying to figure out how to make Jack perform that they did not see Butch sneak in. He dashed onto the stage.

"Butch!" Jack exclaimed.

"Shhh! Jump on my back and let's get out of here."

The people turned and saw them. "After them!" shouted the man. "They're getting away!"

With Jack on his back, Butch ran out the back door and took off down the sidewalk.

Jack held on tight. What a ride!

18

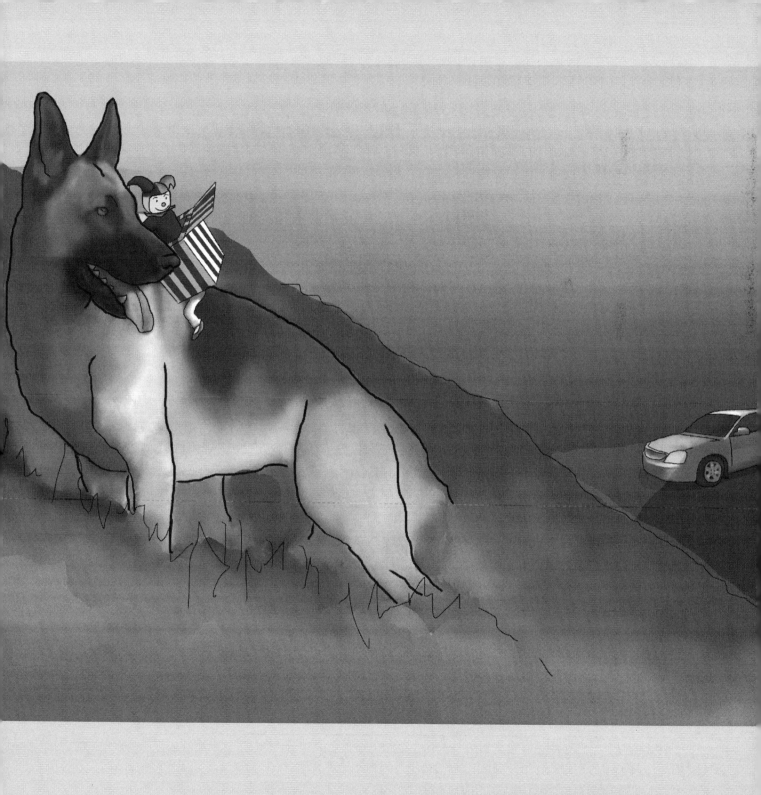

The pursuers ran after them. "Stop! Stop!"

Butch took a shortcut through the woods and back to the sidewalk. The man and woman hurried back to their car and soon caught up with them.

"Faster, Butch! They're catching us!" cried Jack.

Butch darted off the sidewalk and behind a house. The man swerved the car onto the sidewalk and hit a telephone pole.

That stopped them - but only for a minute. They got out of the car and ran after Butch and Jack. When they reached the back of the house a big Rottweiler chased them. They scrambled over a fence and fell into a pond on the other side. Now they were wet and muddy.

Butch kept running. Jack held on tight.

After what seemed a hundred miles, they arrived at Shane's front door. Butch barked. Jack yelled, "Open up in there. I'm home!"

The door opened. There stood Jim and Julie.

"Jack!"

"How did you get home?"

"This is Butch. He saved me! What a ride we had!"

Jack jumped off the dog's back. "Thank you, Butch. I'll never forget you."

"I'll never forget you, either," barked Butch as he turned and ran home. He was glad Jack's adventure was over.

Jack said, "Where's Shane?"

"In his room," said Julie, "but you cannot see him until Jim and I have a serious talk with you. Now into your box for a while."

Julie pushed him into his box and set him in the corner. But he didn't go quietly. He went kicking and screaming!

Later, when Julie let him out of his box, he said, "I hate it when you push me back in my box. I want to stay out!"

"We put you in there when we don't like your behavior, Mr. Jack-in-the-Box! Where did you go? Do you know you broke Shane's heart?"

Jack hung his head. "I've been a very bad toy. I saw the lights of the city from the yard and decided I had to go there. Two mean people captured me and tried to make me sing and dance in a puppet show! I know now, I have to obey the rules. And I miss Shane."

Shane appeared in the hallway.

Jack scurried over. "Guess who's home? Jack!"

Shane picked him up and hugged him. He pushed Jack into his box, turned the handle - and out popped Jack!

Jack sprouted his legs and ran, and Shane ran after him.

Jim said to Julie, "I'm glad to have that obnoxious little squirt back!"

Julie laughed. "Me, too!"

A short while later Grandmother came over. She watched Shane and Jack play, and remembered how Julie played with the same toy years ago. Maybe, she said to herself, when Shane is all grown up, he will be the father of a boy or a girl - and that child too will like to play with Mr. Jack-in-the-Box.

The End

Made in the USA
Las Vegas, NV
26 November 2023